PUFFIN BOOKS

TALON THE FALCON

Deepak Dalal gave up a career in chemical engineering to write stories for children. He lives in Pune with his wife, two daughters, and several dogs and cats. He enjoys wildlife, nature and the outdoors. All his stories have a strong conservation theme. His earlier books in the VikramAditya adventure series are set in India's wilderness destinations. This is his first book in the Feather Tales series.

DEEPAK DALAL

Talon the Falcon

Illustrations by
Lavanya Naidu

PUFFIN BOOKS

PUFFIN BOOKS

USA | Canada | UK | Ireland | Australia
New Zealand | India | South Africa | China

Puffin Books is part of the Penguin Random House group of companies
whose addresses can be found at global.penguinrandomhouse.com

Published by Penguin Random House India Pvt. Ltd
7th Floor, Infinity Tower C, DLF Cyber City,
Gurgaon 122 002, Haryana, India

Penguin
Random House
India

First published in Puffin Books by Penguin Random House 2016

Copyright © Deepak Dalal 2016
Illustrations by Lavanya Naidu

ISBN 9780143427902

Book design and layout by Neelima P Aryan
Printed at Replika Press Pvt. Ltd, India

www.penguinbooksindia.com

Chapter 1
Where Are the Birds?

Shikar, the squirrel, rested in his nest, high above the ground, in the old jacaranda tree. It was yet another one of those bright, cloudless days at the Rose Garden. Shikar was a cheerful squirrel, always happy on such days. But, for some reason, he was uneasy today. It was during his morning play, when he had been dashing spiritedly all over the Rose Garden, that he had sensed not all was well. Something about the place disturbed him. The squirrel furrowed his brow, wondering what the bother was.

Kabul, the bulbul, nested above Shikar in the same tree. Kabul was the wisest bird of the garden. When troubled, the squirrel always sought the bulbul's guidance. As he had done several times in the past hour, Shikar lifted his head. But Kabul's nest was empty.

Shikar turned his gaze to the garden, searching for his other bird friends. Where was Blackpie, the chirpy, happy-go-lucky magpie-robin? There was no sign of Mysun either. Come rain or shine, every morning, the little sunbird hovered among the roses, seeking the sweetest nectar that only his long beak could pry from those delicate blooms.

Birds thronged the Rose Garden at this time of day, feeding in its trees and in its grasses, and frolicking in its sunlit glades. But there were no mynas today, no bulbuls, no koels, no bee-eaters, no ioras, no babblers. There wasn't a single bird in the Rose Garden. A deep silence pervaded the trees; their branches were still and empty.

Shikar sat up. This was odd. Extremely odd! Now that Shikar thought of it, even Lovey and Dovey, the inseparable doves, hadn't stopped by for their morning feed. Shikar couldn't recall a single morning they had failed to visit.

The sharp aroma of human food distracted Shikar. The squirrel gazed down at the human den at the centre of the garden. Its doors were wide open, as they always were at this time of day. Wow-Wow, the dog, was slouched in his usual corner, balefully eyeing Shikar. All was well in the human den. Just another morning.

In the garden, butterflies fluttered and bumblebees droned. But there was no joyful singing of birds. In the trees and on the grass, there was a strange hush.

Shikar rose and slipped noiselessly along the branches of the jacaranda tree. A tangle of leaves and shrubs bordered the garden and, skipping from one to another, he wound a path through them. The boundary

wall of the Rose Garden drew near and when it slid beneath him, he entered the neighbouring Leaf Garden. He searched the trees for Skee, the bee-eater, and Sailor, the tailorbird, who lived here. But, in this garden, too, there were no birds.

The squirrels of the Leaf Garden were home, however. Khismis and Elaichi, the parents of his best friends, were eyeing him disdainfully. Ignoring them, Shikar hunted for their children, Paan and Supari. He found them resting among the giant leaves of a banana tree.

'Hi!' greeted Shikar, bouncing on the leaf.

The squirrels did not return his greeting.

'Where are all the birds?' chattered Shikar. 'I cannot find them. Where have they gone?'

Paan and Supari glanced nervously about them.

'*Quiet!*' hissed Paan. 'Don't talk so loudly.'

Shikar stared at Paan in amazement. He opened his mouth to let Paan have a piece of his mind but Supari, his sister, spoke.

'There,' she whispered, turning her pretty snout to the human den of the Leaf Garden. 'That is the reason why all the birds have flown away.'

Shikar looked.

In the veranda of the den, squatting as if in mid-air, was a bird. This was no ordinary bird; it was the biggest and most fearsome bird that Shikar had ever seen. It perched proudly on talons so large that they sent shivers snaking down Shikar's spine. A casual slash would rip a squirrel to shreds—no question about it. As Shikar watched, the bird cocked its head. Its eyes swung towards the squirrels and settled on them. Paan and Supari squealed with fright, and Shikar's heart started

to hammer woodpecker-like in his chest. Shikar's friends fled the banana tree and cowered behind a bush. Paan began to sob helplessly. Shikar tore his eyes from the gaze of the frightful bird and joined his friends in the bushes.

Supari stood shaking beside her sobbing brother. 'Th-that is a falcon,' she stuttered.

'A falcon?' asked Shikar.

'You don't know about falcons?' Supari stared at Shikar. 'They are monster birds. Crueller than even monitor lizards. They swoop down from the sky and seize us in their terrible talons. They kill everything—birds, too. That is why your bird friends have flown away. Like us, they, too, are terrified of the falcon.'

'Why doesn't it go away?' wailed Paan. 'Fly back to the forests it came from?'

There was a sudden chattering call.

'Paan, Supari—come back here!' It was the squirrels' mother, Khismis. 'How many times have I told you not to play with that bird-squirrel? Come here this instant! No chit-chatting or fooling around with him while the falcon is in this garden.'

Paan and Supari's parents did not like Shikar. For that matter, all the squirrels of the Leaf Garden disliked

Shikar. The root of their ill feeling towards him was his features—his startlingly white face, which was so unlike their elegant brown ones. Then there was his friendship with the birds. They distrusted Shikar for speaking the bird language. No squirrel had ever learnt it before. But Shikar, whose parents had died when he was an infant, had been brought up by Kabul, the wise bulbul. Kabul had taught him the ways of the birds, their language and their songs. Squirrels, as a rule, dislike birds, and the squirrels of the garden deplored Shikar's friendship with them. Every squirrel was deeply suspicious of Shikar— all except his two friends, Paan and Supari.

Shikar flicked his tail. 'You two better return before your mother gets angry. And stop crying, Paan. The falcon is bound to go away soon.'

Chapter 2
The Falcon

Shikar was curious about the falcon. After his friends departed, he emerged from the bush for a closer look. Shikar gulped, regretting his decision instantly. He shivered as his body turned cold all over. Every feature of the bird—every feather, every curve, every slant of monstrous head and body—inspired a fear so terrible that it iced the blood in his veins. Those mighty wings! That powerful neck! Those piercing eyes! That horrible hooked beak!

The falcon sat deathly still, staring sternly at the bird-squirrel.

Shikar trembled. Those eyes! So large, so unblinking. It was as if the eyes of the falcon were casting a spell on him. Something strange was happening to Shikar. He felt as if he was no longer in control of his legs. One by

one, his tiny paws moved, drawing him out of the shelter of the bushes, dragging his unwilling body towards the bird. Shikar wanted to flee. But the blazing eyes of the falcon lured him on. Shikar crawled through the grass, drawn like a helpless moth to a flame.

The squirrels of the Leaf Garden watched with bated breath. Supari sobbed as she saw her dearest friend heading for what seemed to be his certain doom.

'Now you know why I tell you never to play with that bird-squirrel,' whispered Khismis to her children. 'He would have taken you along with him to the falcon.'

'The falcon will skin him,' hissed Elaichi. 'It will tear him apart and swallow him alive!'

Supari and Paan looked on in horror. But Shikar was unaware of his friends. He was unconscious of everything except the two dazzling circles of light that drew him forward.

The bird did not move, nor did it blink its smouldering eyes. Shikar had reached the veranda now. He crawled across the cool stone of the human den. The bird towered over him. He could smell its harsh odour. Its barbed talons were like fierce thorns, and its beak was hooked and cruel. Suddenly, Shikar came to a halt. A mournful melody pierced the haze that muddled his mind. A dismal voice, rich and deep, droned above him:

9

This cage,

This awful creation of man.

Barred from freedom, forever I am.

No sunlight, no moonlight, no starlight for me.

No sky, no cloud, no wind.

No wingbeat, no heartbeat,

No freedom, no life.

No, don't look at me, surely you'll cry,

For never again shall I reach for the sky.

This cage,

This sinful reflection of man.

Barred from freedom, forever I am.

O evil cage, thief of birds' souls,

In this most terrible prison, my wings entombed.

Oh, if you see me, surely you'll cry,

For never again shall I reach for the sky.

No desert, no mountain, no river, no sea.

No whirling, no twirling, no swirling for me.

No wingbeat, no heartbeat,

No freedom, no life.

Oh, if you see me, surely you'll cry,

For never again shall my wings reach for the sky.

Shikar blinked. The spell was broken. He quailed when he realized where he stood. He was in the human den and, worse still, under this fearsome bird. The squirrel panicked. But as he spun to bolt back to the garden, he heard the words of the mournful song once more.

Shikar looked at the falcon. Indeed, there was a cage around him. Thin, pale bars imprisoned the bird, preventing him from soaring to the skies he so dearly loved.

Shikar was keenly aware that the bird would have torn him to shreds if there had been no cage to hold it back. Yet Shikar's little heart went out to the unfortunate bird as he sang his sad song over and over again. His circumstances were tragic. His mighty wings—his most precious possession—the human cage had chained, reducing them to stumps of feather and bone. It was the most crushing fate that could befall a winged creature.

Shikar blurted out before he could stop himself. 'If I help you,' he squeaked, 'will you promise never to harm me or my friends?'

The singing ceased abruptly. Shikar trembled as the falcon swung his mighty neck.

'A squirrel that can speak the bird language!'

exclaimed the bird in a deep, booming voice. 'Blow my feathers away! In all my travels, I, Talon the falcon, have never come across a squirrel who can speak our language.'

'I have sharp teeth,' chattered Shikar. 'They can cut through the twine that binds the door of your cage!'

Talon looked attentively at him. 'But why would you want to help me? I am a bird that swallows squirrels for breakfast.'

Shikar scrabbled up a nearby wall till he was level with the falcon. 'The birds and squirrels of our gardens are terrified of you. Every bird has fled, and my squirrel friends refuse to play. If you promise to return to your forests and to never harm me or my friends, I will help you.'

'*I PROMISE!*' squawked Talon. 'If you free my wings and return me to the skies, I vow to never harm a squirrel again. I pledge my wings, too—the most supreme oath a bird can take. May Greatbill tear my wings off me if ever I slay a squirrel.'

Shikar stared at the bird. Hunter and prey gazed at one another.

Shikar did not pause to consider the consequences of his actions. It mattered not to him that he planned

13

to set free a creature that could kill and devour him. He thought only of the horrible fate of imprisonment, a most terrible wrong that he had to set right.

The squirrel leapt from the wall on to the cage. But even as he wrapped his feet around the bars, he heard a shuffling sound from the human den.

A human emerged. It was Chintu, the awful human youngster who lived in the Leaf Garden. His face was grimy and sticky, smeared liberally with a substance that glittered in the sunlight. The boy's ample stomach jiggled as he lumbered towards the cage. His eyes flashed when he spotted Shikar.

'SHOO! You squirrel!' he shouted, raising a grubby hand and running to the cage. 'Leave my bird alone!'

Shikar leapt to the ground. He darted through the grass, with the plump boy giving chase. Reaching a tree, Shikar sped up its trunk.

Chintu's father had stepped out to see what the matter was.

'That white-headed squirrel!' exclaimed Chintu heatedly. 'He was sitting on the falcon's cage. I shooed the ugly devil away.'

Chintu's father was not as wide around the waist as

his son. But what he lacked in width, he made up in height. He was a tall, heavyset man. Although not as obese as Chintu, flesh hung from him in deep, crumpled folds. So pulpy was his face that his eyes were no more than slits.

Those slits, at that moment, were dark and angry. 'I want no animal or bird coming near my magnificent falcon!' he snarled. 'Watch over him carefully, Chintu; he is your responsibility.' The big man glowered at his son. 'If the bird is harmed, I will spank you. You understand?'

Oddly, instead of alarming the boy, the harshly spoken words had the opposite effect. Chintu puffed his big chest like a bird. 'No need to worry, Dad,' he smirked. '*I* will protect the falcon.'

Chintu's father crossed to the cage and gazed proudly at the fettered bird. 'You, my dear falcon, are my most prized possession. My friends—' he paused to snigger, 'they make do with parrots, lovebirds and munias. Wishy-washy birds that can harm only flies. Only *I* have a real bird—a hunter, a warrior, a killer . . . a falcon.' He drew closer, his face almost touching the cage. 'And what a magnificent falcon you are! A prize worthy of kings. Arab sheikhs would shell out a fortune

for you. But rest easy, my beauty, for I will never part with you. You will be mine forever. My friends will yearn for a bird like you, and I will draw great pleasure from their yearning. This cage will be your home for life and you shall be my favourite pet.'

Shikar panted, watching the humans from the safety of a tree. The fat boy gesticulated angrily at him. Talon the falcon began to sing his mournful song. The big human settled in a chair under the cage, admiring the bird as it sang.

'Look at your bird-squirrel friend,' scolded Khismis, as Shikar stole back into the Rose Garden. 'He is a playmate of the dreaded falcons, too. He is untrustworthy—a fake squirrel, a white-headed impostor. Haven't I always told you so?'

Chapter 3
Blackpie Returns

Back in the Rose Garden, Shikar discovered that his friend Blackpie had returned. So accustomed had he grown to strange behaviour that day that it did not surprise him to find the playful robin cowering inside a bougainvillea bush.

'Where have you been?' demanded Shikar. 'I have been searching for you birds all day.'

Blackpie backed away. 'Quiet!' he whispered. 'There is a falcon in the Leaf Garden and—'

'I know,' interrupted Shikar, and Blackpie, his beak agape, listened in amazement as his snow-faced friend related his story.

'The falcon is in a man-made cage and can do you no harm,' concluded Shikar. The squirrel did not mention

his unsuccessful attempt at rescuing the falcon. 'Listen . . . you can hear him singing his sad song.'

The faint notes of the sorrowful verses came lilting through the trees. Blackpie cocked his head and, as he heard the words, he sang along:

This cage,

This awful creation of man.

Barred from freedom, forever I am.

No sunlight, no moonlight, no starlight for me.

No sky, no cloud, no wind.

No wingbeat, no heartbeat,

No freedom, no life.

No, don't look at me, surely you'll cry,

For never again shall I reach for the sky.

O Greatbill, O grand ruler of Sky!

O Greatbill, you gifted us wings,

Wings so wondrous to wander the world.

Wings so strong to soar the skies.

Wings so priceless, of feathers so fine.

Wings so precious, only for birds.

This cage,

This sinful reflection of man.

Barred from freedom, forever I am.

O evil cage, thief of birds' souls,

In this most terrible prison, my wings entombed.

Oh, if you see me, surely you'll cry,

For never again shall I reach for the sky.

No desert, no mountain, no river, no sea.
No whirling, no twirling, no swirling for me.
No wingbeat, no heartbeat,
No freedom, no life.
Oh, if you see me, surely you'll cry,
For never again shall my wings reach for the sky.

Shikar gazed in wonder at his friend. 'How do *you* know the song?' he queried.

The magpie-robin sighed. 'The song is the lament of a bird that has lost its freedom. All caged birds sing this song.'

They listened in silence while the sorrowful chant was crooned over and over again.

Blackpie picked nervously at the feathers on his chest. 'I feel for him,' he chirruped. 'Wings are everything for us birds. They are our life, our soul. They are more vital than even our hearts. With wings, we fly; we enjoy the freedom of the skies. A cage steals that freedom from us. It stills our wingbeat forever. When that happens, our heartbeat follows and also ceases one day. Next time you see a caged bird, look closely. The bird is alive but its heart is dead. No wingbeat, no heartbeat. All winged creatures dread the ghastly fate that has befallen the falcon. I do not wish it on any bird—not even on a falcon.'

It was then that Shikar spoke of his failed bid to rescue the falcon.

Blackpie was indignant. '*You* tried to free a *falcon*?' he cried.

Shikar defended himself. 'You yourself say that no bird should be caged. And besides, Talon promised never to attack any of the birds or squirrels of the gardens.'

Wings swished the air as the friends argued. A branch shook as a bulbul settled beside them. Kabul had arrived! Though careful not to show his feelings, Shikar was thrilled that the bulbul had returned. Kabul's presence always calmed Shikar. Hope warmed his bosom like a summer breeze. Kabul would sort things out. Soon, everything would be fine.

Kabul patiently heard Blackpie and Shikar out. After careful consideration, she judged Shikar to be right. 'The falcon uttered the supreme oath, pledging his wings,' chirped the bulbul. 'That oath is never taken lightly. Birds of prey are birds of honour too; they never go back on their word. The falcon has promised not to attack us, and so it is our duty to rescue him. Besides, falcons can be valuable friends. They don't forget favours. Talon will help us when we are in need.'

Blackpie started to argue but Kabul would have none of it. She declared that they would free the falcon and, since the presence of the bird was unsettling, they would attempt to liberate Talon that night itself.

The Fountain

News spread quickly that the falcon was caged and as the day progressed, Shikar's bird friends returned to the gardens. By evening, most were back and when Paani-wallah, the mali, switched on the fountain, they gathered on its graceful stone ledges to swap tales and slake their thirst.

Kabul was the first bird to alight on the fountain. While she drank her fill, dipping her beak in the cool, flowing water, Bongo, the black bird with the V-shaped tail, and Skee, the green bee-eater, arrived. Soon, Mysun, the tiny sunbird with the absurdly long beak, flew in, his gaudy feathers flashing in the evening sun.

The fountain was located at the centre of a large, grassy lawn. Although his bird friends could effortlessly wing across to the fountain, for Shikar the journey wasn't

so straightforward. The squirrel had to descend from the trees and cross the open spaces of the lawn to get there. This shouldn't have been a bother but in Shikar's case, there was a problem. When on the ground, there was always trouble for him: an obstacle in the form of a big, slobbering dog with evil intentions—Wow-Wow.

Looking down from his perch high up on a mango tree, Shikar spotted Wow-Wow. The dog was at his usual evening post beside the fountain, guarding it. He sat alert, head up, his bloodshot eyes fixed on Shikar. Shikar grinned and made a rude face at the dog. Next, he shifted his gaze to the human den. Sure enough, the human girl was at the large window. Like Wow-Wow, she, too, was staring up at him.

The stage was set for the evening ritual. Shikar prepared to make the hazardous crossing to the fountain. Wow-Wow stiffened, ready to pounce on the squirrel. The human girl watched, wondering how the white-headed squirrel would outwit the dog. And as they wallowed in the fountain waters, Shikar's bird friends discussed the possible pranks the squirrel might pull.

'Think he'll charge the dog?' queried Skee the bee-eater.

Kabul shook her wise head. 'He had better not. I've warned him against that stupid ploy. The last time he tried that, the dog almost bit his head off. Shikar laughs it off, but it will be the end of him if he makes a mistake. That dog might be foolish but his intentions are evil.'

Just then, Blackpie the magpie-robin shot into view in a blur of flashing wings. Speeding across the lawn, he swooped on the dog. Dropping low, the robin shrieked a rhythmic, thumping kind of noise.

'Hey!' squawked Skee. 'We've heard that before!'

Every bird in the gardens was familiar with the clanging sound that Blackpie was mimicking. It was the tom-tomming of a spoon on a plate—the noise the humans used to signal Wow-Wow that his meal was ready. Blackpie was imitating the sound to perfection.

The effect on the dog was comical. Wow-Wow froze in mid-bark. His floppy ears shot skyward, and his tail stiffened like a hairy stick. He spun in one blurry motion. Then he took off with a giant leap. In three bounds, Wow-Wow crossed the lawn. The birds and the girl lost sight of him as he turned the corner of the human den, and when they heard frenzied yelping and a great thumping, they knew that the dog had reached the kitchen door. The thumping grew loud and frantic, and was soon accompanied by a wailing whine.

Back in the garden, thanks to Blackpie, Shikar's path was clear. He descended the mango tree, his tiny body quaking with mirth. Trotting unmolested across the lawn, he joined his friends on the fountain.

28

Squawking exultantly, Blackpie touched down beside Shikar. With a flourish that would have done a preening peacock proud, the magpie-robin bowed. The squirrel rocked on his haunches and leaned his head forward. Blackpie lowered his beak. A hard, smooth beak gleefully stroked a soft, furry head.

When their jubilation subsided, Kabul hopped across to them. She spoke to Blackpie, her expression stern. 'A laugh at the dog's expense is fine . . . but I would have you know that the prank you pulled on Mysun was in extremely poor taste.'

'Oh, come on, Kabul,' twittered Blackpie, 'I was only having fun.'

'*FUN?*' screeched a high-pitched voice. Mysun the sunbird streaked forward like a burst of sunlight and hovered beside Blackpie. 'You call that *fun?* Promising me that the falcon is gone and then tricking me into flying straight at him? I almost fell to the ground when

29

I saw that frightful bird. I couldn't breathe. I must have shed countless feathers, and it's all because of you and your fun!'

Shikar always sided with Blackpie when it came to making fun of Mysun. 'Hey,' squeaked the squirrel. 'You're short-sighted, Mysun. Don't accuse Blackpie. It's all that nectar you swallow. Makes you like a bee, you know. Your eyesight is even worse than a bee! It's not Blackpie's fault you can't see.'

'Yes,' squawked Blackpie. 'Those bars were shining in the sun. You had to be blind not to have seen them. But all your little bee-brain sees is flowers, right? Don't blame you, of course, considering you flit among them all day.'

'That's enough!' snapped Kabul. 'No more beak from you, Blackpie; and you stay out of it, Shikar. You know very well that the sight of a falcon is confusing. Falcons scare the very feathers off our wings, so that all we see is the bird and not the cage. You are nothing but a sham, Blackpie. Weren't you the first to flee when you noticed the falcon this morning? Everyone saw you. You've gotten over your fright because you heard his cage-song. What you did to Mysun wasn't fair at all.'

'Aw, forget it, Kabul,' said Bongo the drongo. 'It was just a prank.' He turned to the indignant, hovering sunbird. 'Drop it, Mysun. It's been sorted now. There are other, more important things to talk about.'

'Yes,' piped Skee. 'Like what are we going to do about the falcon? Now that I'm over my fright, I see the cage and the bars that imprison it. But that doesn't stop me from shedding feathers every time I look at it.'

'And what about its lament?' asked Bongo. 'That horrid cage-bird lament sears my soul.' Bongo paused, shuddering. 'It's terrible. A bird that lives but its heart is dying. The falcon's sorrow is worse than even death. I can't take it! Its lament rings in my ears.'

Kabul nodded her feathered head. 'Yes. My heart bleeds for its condition. What a horrible fate!'

'I'd rather not live,' squawked Skee. The bee-eater shivered so hard that feathers tumbled from his wings. 'You're right, Kabul. No bird, not even a kill-bird like a falcon, should have to suffer like this.'

Skee straightened his emerald-green head. 'Flight!' he shrilled, flapping his wings and shooting to the sky, 'Greatbill's divine gift to us.' He screeched and somersaulted back to the fountain. 'Humans are worse

than falcons; they're worse than even cats. Falcons and cats go about their business of killing with speed and honesty. It's over and done with. But cheating us out of flight . . . it's the worst death imaginable. No wingbeat, no heartbeat. The heart of a bird dies when its wings are caged.'

Mysun quit his hovering and dropped to the fountain. 'You mean the falcon can never fly again?' croaked the little sunbird.

Blackpie flitted to Mysun's side. Bending, he peered attentively into the sunbird's ear. 'That's odd,' he said. 'There's nothing there.'

'Eh?' blinked Mysun. 'What are you looking for?'

'There's something in your ear,' said the magpie-robin. 'Your hearing must surely be blocked. All we've been talking about is the falcon and its imprisonment, but you haven't got it.'

'Of course he didn't get it,' said Shikar. 'Mysun's hearing is permanently blocked. There's pollen inside his ears! It's too fine for you to see, Blackpie—like dust. But it's there all right.'

Mysun stared perplexedly at Shikar and Blackpie, *still* not getting it.

'Oh, quit it, you two,' said Bongo. He turned to Mysun and spoke patiently. 'The falcon can never fly again, Mysun. The bird is caged.'

'Oh!' blurted Mysun. His hooked beak popped open. 'That's terrible . . . horrible! The poor falcon! O Greatbill, that's a fate I wouldn't wish on any bird; not even a falcon.'

Shikar started to say something but Kabul silenced him with a furious stare. She then turned her gaze to Blackpie, and the robin dutifully dropped his head. More than their teasing of Mysun, Kabul was worried that Shikar and Blackpie might reveal their plans for the night. The three of them had decided earlier that they would not breathe a word about their night-time venture. Kabul was certain that their plans would agitate their friends, so much so that the birds might force them to abandon their rescue attempt—an outcome that Blackpie might have been content with, but not Shikar, nor she.

Kabul steered the discussion to other subjects. Turning to Bongo, she asked, 'Any news of the doves Lovey and Dovey?'

'I met them in the forest,' said Bongo. 'The falcon scared them away in the morning.' The black drongo

turned to the squirrel, his forked tail-feathers shimmering in the sunlight. 'Shikar, I have to tell you, the doves were terribly worried for you.'

Shikar's eyes sparkled. 'That's sweet of them. I missed them this morning.'

'They should be back tomorrow,' said Kabul. 'I am sure they know of the cage by now. The news has spread. What other tidings, Bongo?'

On matters relating to bird news and gossip, there was no better source of information than Bongo. Unlike the other birds, who spent most of their day near the gardens, Bongo flew away each morning to the wires. This was an area where humans had erected many poles and had strung wires on them. The birds collected on the wires in large numbers to chat and exchange news. The drongo never missed a day at the wires, and so birds always turned to him when they sought news.

'The great migrations have begun,' said the black bird. 'Heard the story in the morning. The northern freeze is setting in and the southern departures are underway.'

'Really?' shrilled Shikar. 'Does that mean—'

'Yes, Shikar,' said Kabul. 'That would mean Longtail

has begun his journey. But don't get your hopes up. His migration takes weeks as he has to travel from the far north. Besides, he's a skybird[*] and so, he has to halt at Birdpur. Goodness knows, but the bird council there always has an assignment for him. So there's still plenty of time for him to return.'

From behind her windowpane, the human girl watched the birds till the sky turned pink. As twilight yielded to dusk, she watched them disperse, winging to their roosts in the trees. Her favourite creature, the snow-headed squirrel, was the last to leave. Wow-Wow the dog had been punished—leashed to his kennel for the ruckus he had created. And so the squirrel descended unchallenged and tramped safely to his home in the jacaranda tree.

---

[*]Skybirds ensure law and order amongst birds. They are police-like birds.

chapter 4
Nightfall

The gloom of night is not a happy time for birds and squirrels. Darkness confuses them. Shadows bother them. Even the rustling of leaves in the wind can frighten them. So, as dusk yields to night and stars spark the skies, they bed down to dream of the sun and its comforting light and of happy times.

There would be no dreams for three small creatures that night, however. Shikar, Kabul and Blackpie sat quietly in the jacaranda tree. Huddling, they watched the lights of the human den wink out one by one. Finally, every light was extinguished and there was darkness in the garden. Stars twinkled and a bright moon shone in the night sky. A lizard chattered loudly from the shadows of the human den.

Kabul stirred. The Rose Garden had settled for the

night; it was time to check whether the Leaf Garden had quieted down too. She clicked her beak to draw the attention of the others. Then she rose into the darkness with a flutter of wings. Though afraid, the bulbul mastered her nervousness well, swallowing it like she would a worm. A bat clicked loudly, and Kabul swerved in mid-flight as the wraith-like creature shot past. Soon Kabul was high enough to gaze down at the Leaf Garden. Except for the moon, no light illuminated the garden's shadowed expanse.

Returning to the jacaranda tree, Kabul touched down, her wings rustling softly. 'It's quiet in the Leaf Garden,' she whispered. 'No one there. Time for you to get moving, Shikar. Be careful. Cross the wall, and join Blackpie and me at the jackfruit tree. We'll wait for you there.'

Kabul poked Shikar affectionately with her beak. Although Kabul was calm and composed, Blackpie had turned nervous. The robin shuffled awkwardly, not looking Shikar in the eye. The birds rose to the sky and Shikar, ruing the absence of wings, wended his way across the wall.

Leaves rustled as the squirrel crawled from one branch to another. His little heart skipped a beat when a fuzzy shadow flitted across his path. Shikar froze, but

the creature slithered away with a sharp crackling. He resumed his journey, his chest heaving furiously. Without any further incident, he reached the tree where the two birds were waiting.

The jackfruit tree stood at the edge of an untidy lawn, where there were more weeds than grass. The human den was visible from its branches, and the three friends gazed at the falcon and the cage imprisoning the bird. Moonlight flooded the veranda, its pale light reflecting eerily off the bars of the cage. Though the bird's condition rendered it less harmful than even a butterfly, Kabul and Blackpie quivered at its very sight. Shikar staved off his fright by staring at the metallic twine that fastened the door of the cage. Squirrels have strong teeth; it was Shikar's job to chew and slice the cord.

Kabul pecked Shikar's cheek gently, wishing him luck. 'May Greatbill be with you,' she whispered. 'Take care. And don't worry. Blackpie and I are watching over you.'

Shikar descended silently. His heart was thumping so loudly that he feared it would wake the entire neighbourhood. When he reached the ground, an unsettling expanse of weed and grass—open to the sky—stretched before him. Crickets chirruped in the

bushes. Bats circled the human den, clicking loudly. Shikar's tail grew stiff as it always did when he was nervous. Even during the day, squirrels are wary of open spaces; in the darkness, he had to summon all his courage to abandon the shelter of the trees. Swallowing his fear, Shikar advanced slowly through the grass. The long shadow of the human den drew closer. When the squirrel was halfway to the den, the grass ahead rustled threateningly. He heard a loud squeak.

A rat!

Shikar froze as the blades parted and the face of a hairy animal appeared. As Shikar turned to flee, a flapping noise closed in overhead, terrifying him even more. The rat squeaked in alarm and fled. The flapping pursued the rat. Shikar's nerve abandoned him and, digging his feet into the mud, he buried his head in the grass.

'It's only me!' squawked a voice from above. It was Blackpie. 'Oh, how the rat fled,' cackled the magpie-robin. 'What a sight! I wish you had seen. I flapped my wings like an owl and swooped on him as if he were my dinner.'

Shikar did not find the incident funny at all. His heart was beating so hard in his chest that it hurt. The squirrel had thought that it was *he* who would be the owl's dinner. He wanted to shout at his friend, tell him off for scaring him so, but he kept silent. He was in the midst of a huge open space. What if a real owl chanced upon him?

The Cage

The squirrel resumed his journey with Kabul and Blackpie hovering above him. He scampered through the remaining grass and hopped on to the veranda. The falcon was awake. Shikar could feel the power of his gaze.

'You are the squirrel who tried to rescue me this morning,' whispered Talon in his deep voice. His tone was different now, alive with hope and excitement, like that of a nestling testing its wings for the first time.

'Yes,' replied Shikar. 'I have come to release you.'

Shikar scurried up the wall and leapt on to the cage. Not wasting a moment, he set to work on the twine with his teeth. Kabul and Blackpie hopped to the roof of the house. Kabul twitched her neck nervously. The bats

were worrying her. The creatures seemed to be gathering. The darkness pulsed with their squeaks as they flew in rapid circles above the lawn.

Clinging to the cage, Shikar chewed busily. The twine's wiry strength did not bother the squirrel; he was sure it would part under his teeth. All he needed was time.

Just then, a bat swooped into the veranda and sped to a table beside the cage. Distracted from his work, Shikar turned and saw the bat grab something with its claws. Whatever it was, it slipped and tumbled to the ground. Another bat swept in behind the first. It dived, grabbing the fallen object.

Talon shuffled in his cage. 'You better hurry, my squirrel friend,' he whispered. 'The bats have discovered the food wasted by the humans.'

Soon the veranda was buzzing with bats, and their sharp clicks reverberated throughout the garden. The noise was deafening. The humans would surely emerge to investigate! Shikar worked frantically at the twine. From the roof, Kabul and Blackpie looked on anxiously.

Talon shifted nervously. *The bats!* They could ruin everything. The creatures swarmed in black clouds as they fought for the food, which, by now, was scattered

45

all over the veranda. Talon looked fearfully at the door. His sharp hearing had detected movement inside the den.

'Go, my friend,' he whispered. 'The humans are coming.'

Shikar looked at Talon in dismay.

'Go!' urged the big bird.

A beam of light shone suddenly, blinding Shikar.

'Jump!' squawked Kabul and Blackpie. But Shikar clung to the cage, chewing as fast as he could.

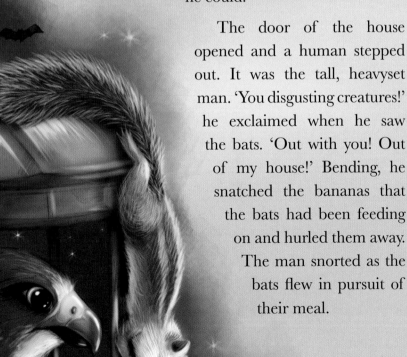

The door of the house opened and a human stepped out. It was the tall, heavyset man. 'You disgusting creatures!' he exclaimed when he saw the bats. 'Out with you! Out of my house!' Bending, he snatched the bananas that the bats had been feeding on and hurled them away. The man snorted as the bats flew in pursuit of their meal.

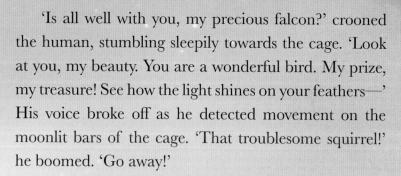

Shikar quaked as he worked. His task was almost done, but was he going to run out of time? He heard footsteps. They were heading for the cage.

'Is all well with you, my precious falcon?' crooned the human, stumbling sleepily towards the cage. 'Look at you, my beauty. You are a wonderful bird. My prize, my treasure! See how the light shines on your feathers—' His voice broke off as he detected movement on the moonlit bars of the cage. 'That troublesome squirrel!' he boomed. 'Go away!'

'Run!' screeched Talon.

'Run!' echoed the birds from the roof.

But Shikar stuck fast to the cage. The man rushed forward, his arm raised to strike the squirrel. But before he could, Shikar squeaked in triumph.

'It's open!' he squealed and leapt for the wall. Shikar fled. He sped to the roof where his friends were waiting.

The human raced after Shikar and shook his fist at the roof, shouting loudly.

From the cage, Talon stared at the human. A cold fire burned in his eyes. He flicked his tongue, stroking the razor-sharp edges of his beak. For birds, beaks are far more than a mere appendage of the mouth, especially in the case of birds of prey, like falcons. For Talon, his beak was his weapon, his sword. Tilting his head, he inclined his beak at a merciless slant. The big bird moved. Extending a wing, he pushed the gate of the cage.

The man heard the cage rattle, and turned. Seeing the gate swing wide, he lunged. But it was too late. At long last, the door to freedom had been opened. It was the bars of the cage that had held Talon captive. The bars had shackled his wings and his soul. And it was the bars that had brewed within him an unspeakable anger. Now he was free, and his rage blazed with the fury of a forest fire. Talon sprang for the human, claws outstretched.

'Help, save me!' screamed the man as he fell to the ground, the bird on top of him. 'Get this awful bird away from me!' he shrieked. The man's fear knew no bounds—and for good reason—for the vengeance of a falcon is terrible. The man stumbled to his feet with Talon clinging on firmly, tearing and slashing with his frightful beak. It was only at the door that the bird released the human. But the man's cries did not cease,

his agonized bawling resounding from inside his den like
the wailing of a terror-stricken child.

Shikar and his friends paid no attention to the human. They gazed at Talon, as the bird hopped on to the veranda wall. The falcon's eyes were aglow. For once, there wasn't a trace of fierceness in them. They were lit, instead, by the light of the purest joy Shikar and his bird friends had ever seen. Roused from a long sleep, Talon's heart had come alive again. Shikar could tell, because the bird's chest was juddering and heaving like a tree in a storm. Talon jubilantly flexed his mighty wings. The wings, that the falcon had despaired of ever

using again, lifted the bird, speeding him joyously to the sky. And as he rose, he sang:

Oh, what a joy,

Oh, what a joy it is to fly.

Greatbill gave us wings to soar to the sky.

Oh, what a joy,

Oh, what a joy it is to fly!

Shikar heard Blackpie and Kabul singing along, and he joined the chorus. The sound of the rapturous singing awoke the birds of the neighbourhood. Their voices spiritedly pitched in, too, and their song reverberated through the night.

Wow-Wow

It was the weekend and Mitalee, the girl who lived in the Rose Garden, was sitting on the garden's lush lawn, beside a bed of rose blooms. Painting was Mitalee's favourite pastime. Currently she was inspired by a splendid yellow rose that had unwrapped its petals to greet the morning sun. Beside her, sprawled Maitreya— her neighbour and school friend—absorbed in a computer game.

Like an expensive rug, Wow-Wow the dog stretched at Mitalee's feet, soaking in the heat of the sun. Although it appeared that the dog was sleeping, Mitalee could see that he wasn't. One eye was half open, like an unfastened shutter, and was fixed on the jacaranda tree. Mitalee turned her gaze to the tree too.

There was the squirrel. He sat on a branch, his

little white head fluffed like cotton in the sunlight. The sight of the squirrel churned a deep longing inside Mitalee. He was so incredibly cute, so cuddly, so adorable, that she wished he were her friend.

But what was the squirrel up to now? The tiny animal had risen. He was on his four legs now, walking down the jacaranda tree

Wow-Wow rolled on to his tummy. His floppy ears perked and a growl escaped his fleshy jowls. His eyes were playing tricks on him—or were they? Wow-Wow blinked. Yes, it was true! That detestable creature, that revolting white-headed worm, was descending to the grass. The cheek of it! How dare that loathsome animal come down while he, the master of the

Rose Garden, sat there? The dog half rose to his feet.

But . . . wait a moment—a rare bolt of inspiration flashed through Wow-Wow's murky brain. His bleary eyes turned redder still. His tongue drooled. This could be the opportunity he yearned for—a chance to get even with this rascally creature! The dog settled back on the grass. He sat tight, not moving a muscle. He wished with all his heart that the foolish animal would keep coming.

The squirrel granted Wow-Wow his wish. The little devil descended cockily, as if he didn't have a care in the world. That maddening smirk, which infuriated Wow-Wow, was stamped all over his face. The squirrel reached the bottom of the tree. He then sauntered on to the grass, striding boldly towards the dog. Mitalee put aside her work. She nudged Maitreya. The boy looked up. He turned still when he saw the squirrel challenging the dog.

Wow-Wow could not believe his luck. The stupid squirrel was actually coming to him! He licked his jaws, and his tail traced slow circles.

Shikar halted barely a metre from the drooling dog. Rising on his hind legs, he stuck his tongue out. This was too much for Wow-Wow. A blood-curdling bark tore loose from him. The dog sprang to his feet.

But as Wow-Wow readied to pounce, the squirrel looked up to the sky. Mitalee, Maitreya and the dog looked too.

The children gasped.

A huge bird was shooting out of the sky! Mitalee quailed in shock. The bird was big—the largest she had ever seen! Its eyes were hard and cold and unimaginably fierce. Its fearsome claws were outstretched, and a dreadful sound trilled from its beak. Wow-Wow squealed in abject terror. The bird was diving at him. He scrabbled desperately, trying pathetically to disappear into the ground.

Talon, however, had no intention of striking the dog. His goal was only to scare the animal, as Shikar had requested of him. Talon swept over the terrified dog, his claws eluding it at the final moment. Yet Wow-Wow was convinced that he had been struck by a hurricane. Howling like a wretched puppy, the dog staggered to his feet. The falcon shrilled his cry once more, as the defeated dog shot into his kennel, his tail tucked between his legs.

Maitreya stared open-mouthed at the falcon, which now wheeling in the air. Beside him, Mitalee was looking at the squirrel. The squirrel's chest

was heaving. His jaws were quivering, as if spouting with uncontrollable mirth. Could squirrels laugh, she wondered? Then she saw the falcon swoop down once more.

Oh no! Was it going to kill the squirrel? Her Snowdrop . . . her beloved, adorable squirrel! She watched in despair as the claws of the big bird wrapped around the squirrel, lifting him off the ground. The bird flexed its wings. Soaring a short distance, it settled on the jacaranda tree, gently dropping the squirrel on one of its branches.

Shikar could not stop laughing. He had not had so much fun in a long time. The agonized whimpering from the kennel was music to his ears.

Blackpie hurtled to where Shikar sat. 'Brilliant!' he squawked. 'Did you hear his squealing? He must have alarmed the entire neighbourhood.'

'He-he-he,' twittered Mysun. The little sunbird had taken time off from his beloved roses to watch the fun. Wow-Wow often troubled him, too, and he was delighted at the dog's humbling.

Several birds had gathered to watch. Lovey and Dovey cooed their applause. Senora, the iora, shook her head. Sailor the tailorbird pranced in glee, and

Skee the bee-eater performed acrobatics in the air. Even Kabul, who rarely approved such eye-for-an-eye tactics, smiled.

'Encore!' screeched Blackpie. 'Once more, Talon. That squealing! We have to hear it again.'

But for Talon, it was time to depart. His fierce eyes had turned tender.

'I must leave for my home in the forests,' he boomed. 'But I will never forget any of you, especially my friend, the bird-squirrel. Together, you have returned to me our most precious gift. My wings beat again and so does my heart. It is because of you that the wind and the skies are mine again.' Talon turned his mighty neck and, even though the fearsome bird was now their friend, several among the bird assembly couldn't help shivering. 'Your wise skybird Kabul and I have spoken. Every bird in these gardens is my friend now. Kabul knows where to find me. You have only to call if you need my help, and I will return. Our sky-paths will surely cross again.'

Talon's mighty wings unfolded and, as he rose gracefully to the sky, the birds of the gardens sang together:

O wind, o mighty wind,

Embrace me again.

Whirl me, twirl me, swirl me,

Lift me to your skies.

O wind, o mighty wind,

My heart and wings, they beat again.

Sunlight, moonlight, starlight,

Paint my wings eternally bright.

O wind, forever you are free,

Across deserts, mountains, rivers and seas.

O wind, restore my wings, revive my soul.

O wind, o mighty wind,

Freedom is forever mine.